Kamal The Muslim Camel. Allah Sees Everything

First published in 2021.
Published by Wow Search Ltd, Sahih Gifts.
Milton Keynes Business Centre,
Foxhunter Drive,
Milton Keynes,
MK14 6DG.

Produced by Sahih Gifts, www.sahihgifts.com

Acknowledgement

I would like to thank my wife Rezia Sultana, for giving me the support and motivation to write this book. She played an important role in helping me to finish this story.

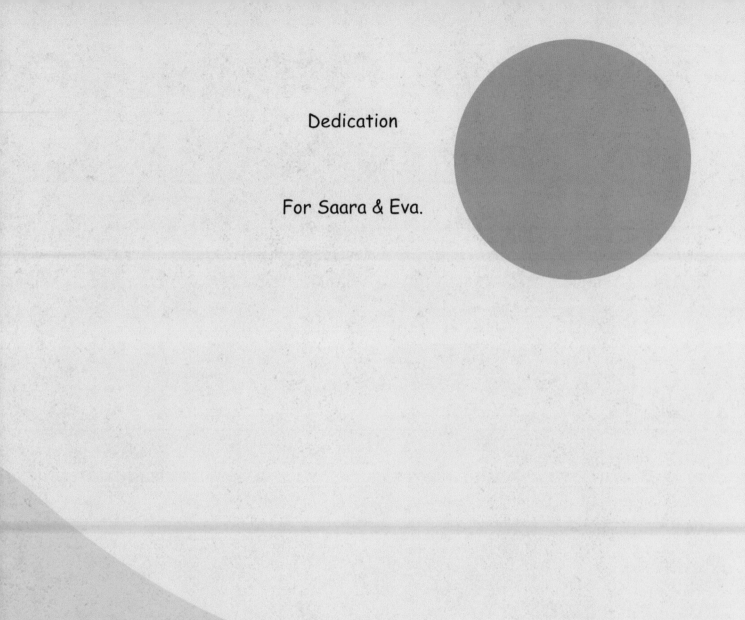

Dedication

For Saara & Eva.

This Kamal The Muslim Camel
book belongs to:

KAMAL THE MUSLIM CAMEL

ALLAH SEES EVERYTHING

AZHAR SOHAIL ISLAM

It was a very hot afternoon in the desert.
Kamal and his friends Kabir and Khadija
were sitting under some date palm trees,
enjoying the shade.

"I'm thirsty; shall we go to the well and
get some water?" asked Kamal.

"Water? Yes, that would help to cool us down.
Let's go," said Kabir and Khadija.

The three friends stood up, shook the sand
of the desert from their bodies,
and started walking slowly towards the well.

When they reached the well, the friends saw that someone had taken the bucket out, meaning they could not get to the cool water inside.

Kamal noticed three sets of footprints and a trail of water droplets leading away from the well. Each of the three trails headed in the direction of one of the three nearby towns where the humans of the area lived.

"Let's go and tell Grandpa Camel," said Kamal. "He will know what to do."

Kabir and Khadija agreed. They both had a worried look on their faces and Kamal was getting very thirsty.

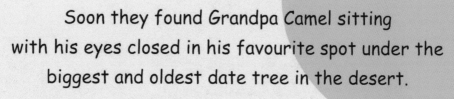

Soon they found Grandpa Camel sitting
with his eyes closed in his favourite spot under the
biggest and oldest date tree in the desert.

"Grandpa, someone has stolen the bucket
from the well and I am very thirsty",
said Kamal excitedly.

Grandpa Camel slowly opened his eyes.
"But there are supposed to be three buckets
at the well. Why didn't you use one of the
other ones?" Grandpa said, pointing at the
pond that he had filled just that
morning.

Kamal, Kabir and Khadija quickly went to
the pond and drank up all the water.

"We are going to have to fill the pond again,"
said Kamal.

"But there are no buckets at the well.
All three have been stolen," Kamal added.

"Don't worry, Kamal," said Grandpa Camel. "I know how you can get the buckets back." Grandpa Camel then told the young camels to go back to the well and follow the footprints. There were three sets of footprints and three of them. Each camel could follow one trail.

"You should be able to find the buckets at the end of each trail of footprints," he said. "Just make sure no one sees you take them back."

Khadija was the first one to come back with a bucket full of water.
She walked to Grandpa's pond and tipped the water into it,
emptying the bucket completely.

Soon Kabir also arrived with a bucket full of water. He, too, emptied all the water into Grandpa's pond, checking that every drop had left the bucket.

The pond was now two thirds full.

"We just need one more bucket of water and the pond will be full," said Grandpa Camel.

Shortly afterwards, Kamal came back to the pond, but he did not have a bucket of water with him.

"Didn't you find the bucket?" asked Grandpa Camel.

Kamal nodded his head. "Oh yes, I did find it. I followed the footprints just like you told me to. The bucket was at the end of the trail. You had asked me to make sure no one was watching and I was about to pick up the bucket (I even had the handles in my mouth!) but then I realised... Allah was watching. He could see everything I was doing, no matter how long I waited for him to turn away or close his eyes. So, I could not take the bucket."

On hearing this Grandpa laughed and said, "When I said to make sure no one was watching, I meant humans."

Kabir and Khadija started to laugh at Kamal's foolishness, but Grandpa told them to stop being so mean.

"It was my fault," he said.

"How was it your fault?" asked Khadija.

"I should have said to make sure no humans were watching. Kamal was actually right and he has also taught us a very important lesson. This is why I always say that Kamal is the best Muslim Camel in the desert. He is always aware of Allah and knows that Allah SWT is always watching and can see him all the time. That is why he never does anything wrong.

"Now take these buckets back to the well so someone else can use them. We can get the other buckets and fill up the pond tomorrow," said Grandpa Camel.

Kamal, Kabir and Khadija put the buckets back at the well and went back to their date trees and fell asleep under the shade.

The end.

Coming soon.

Kamal goes to hajj.

Printed in Great Britain
by Amazon

28420044R00016